From the
Library of:

ALSO BY JUDITH VIORST

Lulu and the Brontosaurus

Lulu's Mysterious Mission

The Tenth Good Thing About Barney

*Alexander and the Terrible, Horrible,
No Good, Very Bad Day*

*My Mama Says There Aren't Any Zombies,
Ghosts, Vampires, Creatures, Demons,
Monsters, Fiends, Goblins, or Things*

Rosie and Michael

*Alexander, Who Used to
Be Rich Last Sunday*

*Alexander, Who's Not (Do You Hear Me?
I Mean It!) Going to Move*

Earrings!

Super-Completely and Totally the Messiest

Just in Case

*If I Were in Charge of the World and Other
Worries: Poems for Children and Their
Parents*

*Sad Underwear and Other Complications:
More Poems for Children and Their Parents*

LULU
Walks the Dogs

JUDITH VIORST

illustrated by LANE SMITH

Atheneum Books for Young Readers
NEW YORK • LONDON • TORONTO • SYDNEY • NEW DELHI

ATHENEUM BOOKS FOR YOUNG READERS
An imprint of Simon & Schuster Children's Publishing Division
1230 Avenue of the Americas, New York, New York 10020

This book is a work of fiction. Any references to historical events, real people, or real places are used fictitiously. Other names, characters, places, and events are products of the author's imagination, and any resemblance to actual events or places or persons, living or dead, is entirely coincidental.

Text copyright © 2012 by Judith Viorst

Illustrations copyright © 2012 by Lane Smith

ATHENEUM BOOKS FOR YOUNG READERS is a registered trademark of Simon & Schuster, Inc.
Atheneum logo is a trademark of Simon & Schuster, Inc.

For information about special discounts for bulk purchases, please contact Simon & Schuster Special Sales at 1-866-506-1949 or business@simonandschuster.com.

The Simon & Schuster Speakers Bureau can bring authors to your live event. For more information or to book an event, contact the Simon & Schuster Speakers Bureau at 1-866-248-3049 or visit our website at www.simonspeakers.com.

Also available in an Atheneum Books for Young Readers hardcover edition

The text for this book is set in Officina Sans.

The illustrations for this book are rendered in pencil on pastel paper.

Manufactured in the United States of America

0515 FFG

First Atheneum Books for Young Readers paperback edition March 2014

10 9 8 7 6 5 4 3 2

The Library of Congress has cataloged the hardcover edition as follows:

Library of Congress Cataloging-in-Publication Data
Viorst, Judith.
Lulu walks the dogs / Judith Viorst ; illustrated by Lane Smith. — 1st ed.
p. cm.
Summary: Lulu needs help from a boy named Fleischman if she is to earn money walking her neighbors' dogs, and she finds out that if she wants her business venture to succeed, she has to be nice.
ISBN 978-1-4424-3579-7 (hardcover)
ISBN 978-1-4424-3581-0 (eBook)
[1. Cooperativeness—Fiction. 2. Dogs—Dogs. 3. Dog walking—Fiction. 4. Moneymaking projects—Fiction.]
I. Smith, Lane, ill. II. Title.
PZ7.V816Luu 2010
[Fic]—dc23
2011023841
ISBN 978-1-4424-3580-3 (pbk)

BOOK DESIGN BY MOLLY LEACH

For Daniel Luoh Hersh

—J. V.

For Strino and Creampuff

—L. S.

SINCE a kid named Fleischman
is going to hang around a whole lot
in these pages, I need to tell you
right away that Fleischman is not his
LAST name but his FIRST name.
Fleischman was his mom's last name
before she married his dad and
changed HER name to HIS, just
like other moms' last names could be

Got it? No? Well,
I'm busy, and it's time to

Anderson or Kelly before THEY got married. (Some moms don't change their last names after they're married, but I really don't feel like discussing that right now.) Anyway—stay with me here—some of these used-to-be Kelly moms might decide to first-name their daughters Kelly, and some Anderson moms might first-name their sons Anderson. Or maybe they'd name their sons Kelly and daughters Anderson. And though not too many Fleischman moms decide to name their kids Fleischman, Fleischman's mom did.

too bad if you don't.
tell my story.

chapter one

Lulu—remember Lulu?—used to always be a big pain, till she met Mr. B, a lovely brontosaurus. Now she is just a sometimes pain, and not nearly as rude as before. But unless what she wants is utterly, totally, absolutely, and no-way-José impossible, she's still a girl who wants what she wants when she wants it.

So, what is it, exactly, that our Lulu wants? Right now I'm just saying it costs a lot of money. Furthermore, her mom and her dad, who give her almost everything she asks for, said to her—with many sighs and sorries—that they couldn't afford to buy it for her and that she would HAVE TO EARN THE MONEY TO GET IT.

Lulu thought about throwing one of her famous screeching, heel-kicking, arm-waving tantrums, except that—since her last birthday—she wasn't doing that baby stuff anymore. So, instead, she tried some other ways—politer, quieter, sneakier, grown-upper ways—of changing their minds.

First try: "Why are you being so cruel to me, to your only child, to your dearest, darlingest Lulu?"

"We're not being cruel," her mom explained in an I'm-so-sorry voice. "You're still our dearest and darlingest. But we don't have the money to spend on things like that."

Second try: "I'll eat only one meal a day and also never go to the dentist, and then you can use all that money you saved to buy it for me."

"Dentists and food are much more important," Lulu's dad explained, "than this thing that you want. Which means"— and here he sighed heavily—"that if you really still want it, you're going to have to pay for it yourself."

Really still want it? Of course she really still wanted it! She was ALWAYS and FOREVER going to want it. But paying for it herself—that might be utterly and totally, plus absolutely and no-way-José, impossible. So she kept on trying to change their minds, making her saddest and maddest and baddest faces and giving her mom and her dad some unbeatable arguments. Like, "I'll move down into the basement, and you'll get the money by renting out my bedroom." Or, "You could get money by selling our car and taking the bus instead, which would also be much better for the environment." But, great as her arguments were, her mom and her dad kept saying no and sighing and sorrying. And after her sixteenth or seventeenth try, Lulu was starting to feel a little discouraged.

Last try: "So, while all the other kids are playing and laughing and having fun, I'll be the only kid my age earning money?"

"Oh, I don't know about that," said Lulu's mom. "That little Fleischman down the street is always earning money by doing helpful chores for folks in the neighborhood. So young and already such a hard-working boy!"

(Well, what do you know, here's Fleischman, and it's only Chapter One. I told you he would be hanging around a lot.)

chapter two

Lulu did not want to hear about hard-working Fleischman. She did not want to hear anything nice about Fleischman. She did not, in fact, want to hear anything about Fleischman. He was such a goody-goody, such a sweet little, kind little, helpful little boy, that Lulu could almost throw up when she heard him soppily say to the lady down at the corner, "You don't have to thank me, Mrs. King. It was an honor to hold your shopping bag." Or, "You paid me too much for raking your leaves, Mr. Rossi. Take back a dollar and keep it for yourself." Yecch! And when, in addition, the neighbors would say how cute, how adorable-looking Fleischman looked, Lulu would secretly wish that he would trip on his shoelace and knock out his front teeth.

Maybe you think that Lulu shouldn't be wishing such wicked wishes. Maybe you're right. But haven't you ever met someone who all the moms and the dads in the world thought was JUST PERFECT, someone you'd never be as perfect as, someone who, no matter what kind of excellent stuff you did, would always do more of it and do it better? (I knew a someone like that when I was a kid, and I still could almost throw up just thinking about her!)

But let's get back to the story.
Lulu needed to make some money.
And she didn't want Fleischman
getting in her way.

So she walked down the street to his
house, where he was sitting on his front
stoop playing his flute, which he did
whenever he wasn't earning money, or
getting the highest marks ever heard of
in school, or being completely adorable
by smiling his dear little smile and saying
to practically everyone he met, "Have a
great—I mean a really great—day." And
his shirt matched his pants, and his pants

matched his socks, and his hair didn't
have one single hair sticking up. Plus, next
to him was a bowl with a snack, and the
snack wasn't Sugar Clusters but sliced
carrots. Just looking at Fleischman made
Lulu so annoyed!

"Here's the deal, Fleischman," she
told him, with her hands on her hips
and her eyebrows scrunched together.
"I won't rake anyone's leaves or carry

their groceries. I won't mail a letter that someone forgot to mail. And in winter I won't help people pour salt on their sidewalks to keep them from slipping on the ice."

"That's interesting," said Fleischman, carefully putting down his flute and smiling his extremely annoying sweet smile. "But what's your point?"

"My point," said Lulu, not smiling back, "is that I'LL stay away from YOUR jobs. But I'm warning you, Fleischman, stay away from MINE."

"Which jobs are those?" asked
Fleischman, getting up from the stoop
and offering Lulu a carrot.

"As soon as I decide," she replied,
waving away the carrot, "I will
tell you."

Lulu went home and thought and
thought, and then she thought some
more, trying to figure out what her jobs
should be. But since the name of this
story I'm telling is *Lulu Walks the Dogs*,
you already know, of course, what
she decided.

chapter three

Well, maybe you already know and maybe you don't. Because maybe Lulu first decided her jobs—or job—should be baking cookies, or spying, or reading to old people, and then those jobs did not turn out too well. And maybe instead of writing a chapter about how those jobs did not turn out too well, I'm moving right along to Chapter Four.

chapter four

Lulu decided that if she got up earlier in the morning she could easily walk a dog before going to school. Somebody in the neighborhood must need a dog walker. Hey, maybe two different somebodies needed a dog walker. Hey, wait a minute, maybe even three. Lulu was certain that she could handle three. And if she charged two dollars and fifty cents a day per dog, and if she walked three dogs five days a week, in one week Lulu could earn . . . (Just give me a moment here—I'll tell you what she could earn. She could earn . . . Don't rush me! Okay—it's thirty-six dollars.)

(Excuse me, it is thirty-seven dollars and fifty cents. I've never been all that great at arithmetic.)

Using her mom's computer and printer, Lulu prepared an announcement that she stuck into all the mailboxes in her neighborhood. Here's what it said:

> LULU THE OUTSTANDING DOG WALKER
> WILL WALK YOUR DOG FOR $2.50 A DAY
> ON MONDAYS, TUESDAYS, WEDNESDAYS,
> THURSDAYS, AND FRIDAYS

Her announcement included her telephone number, so people could give her a call and make an appointment for her and the dog to meet.

By the end of Saturday afternoon, four neighbors had telephoned Lulu. One of these neighbors, however, was—guess who?—Fleischman. "You've got a dog to walk?" Lulu asked grumpily.

"I don't," Fleischman answered. "My mom's allergic to dogs. But I know all about them—I'm sort of kind of an expert. And after I read your announcement I thought that if you'd like, I could give you some advice."

That Fleischman had some nerve,
wanting to give her dog-advice when
he didn't even have a dog of his own!
Although, to be honest, Lulu didn't
either. "Thanks, but no thanks," said Lulu,
in a not-too-thankful voice. "What can be
so hard about walking a dog?"

chapter five

On Sunday, Lulu met three different dogs at three different houses, all in Lulu's neighborhood. Her mom went with her to every house, waiting outside on the sidewalk—just as she always did on Halloween—in case the people inside were witches or ogres. None of them were.

The first dog Lulu met was an enormous, bigheaded, bad-breathed brute named Brutus, who circled around her snarling and sniffing and sniffing and snarling and sniffing while Lulu waved her hand in a cautious hello.

"He's deciding whether he likes you," said Brutus's owner, who looked amazingly like Brutus. "We'll know that he does if he starts thumping his tail."

Lulu quit waving her hand and started saying, "Nice Brutus. Nice Brutus," though she didn't think that Brutus was nice at all. And after he had finally stopped with the circling and sniffing and snarling, and sat himself down in front of her, and glared at her out of his beady bright-red eyes, Lulu quit saying "Nice Brutus" and glared right back. And a little while later, having decided they'd never be New Best Friends, Lulu announced, "Well, I'll be leaving now."

But as Lulu started to leave, Brutus jumped up, ran over, and knocked her flat down on the rug, then proceeded to lick her face and thump his tail. Brutus's owner pumped one fist in the air and announced approvingly, "He likes you. Brutus likes you. He really likes you. And

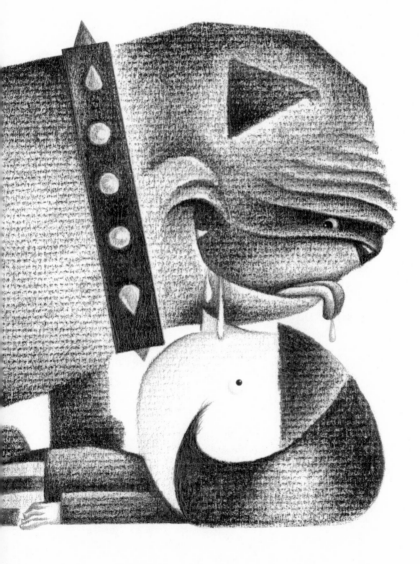

believe me, this is a dog that doesn't like everyone."

"And believe me," said Lulu, standing up and wiping globs of dog-slobber off her face, "I am a girl who also doesn't like everyone."

She was about to add that Brutus was among the everyones she didn't like when his owner said, "You're hired. You're hired. You're definitely hired. And furthermore, because Brutus is on the large side, I'm going to pay you fifty cents extra a day."

(On the LARGE side? Brutus was
GIGANTIC—a mountain, a whale, an SUV
of a dog!)

Still, two dollars and fifty cents and
then another fifty cents made three whole
dollars every single day, which meant that
every five days Lulu would earn, well—after
she figured out what she would earn, she
decided that this was an offer she couldn't
refuse. And so she nodded and said okay
when Brutus's owner said to her, "See you
Monday morning—six thirty sharp."

chapter six

As Lulu walked down the street to her second appointment she started singing this money song, which all of a sudden had popped into her head:

Jimmy, Johnny,
Joseph, Jake.
How much money
will I make?
Laurie, Lucy,
Lynne, LaVerne.
How much money
will I earn?

Money! Money! Money! Money! Money!

By the time she had sung her song
a few times she had come to the next
house, where the doorbell was answered
by someone who introduced herself to
Lulu as Pookie's mommy. (She wasn't a
dog, of course. She was a plump, pink
human being with many curls. Did you
really think that a dog had answered
the doorbell, opened the door, and
introduced herself?)

A teeny-tiny white fuzzball was nestled
cozily against Pookie's mommy's chest
and held in place by Pookie's mommy's
left hand as Pookie's mommy explained
(Hang in there, please—this sentence is
long!) that though her little girl's name

was spelled P-O-O-K-I-E, the POOK part rhymed with DUKE and not with BOOK, and that Pookie got very upset if she was called by a name that rhymed with the wrong word. "You'll never have a problem if you just remember DUKE," said Pookie's mommy—or PUKE, Lulu secretly thought but did not say. "Otherwise, you're sure to hurt her feelings, and trust me, you wouldn't want to hurt Pookie's feelings."

Lulu soon learned that the other thing
that was sure to hurt Pookie's feelings
was expecting Pookie to walk when Lulu
walked her. "Here's how this works,"
Pookie's mommy explained. "*You're* the
one who walks. Pookie gets carried. And
when it's time, you'll sit her, gently,
underneath a tree, and she will do what
she's supposed to do."

"How will I know when it's time?" Lulu

asked. And Pookie's mommy answered, "Not to worry. She will let you know."

During this whole conversation Pookie never opened her eyes, not even when she was handed over to Lulu, who was urged by Pookie's mommy to practice saying Pookie's name several times.

"Nicely done," said Pookie's mommy to Lulu, after she'd finished practicing her OOKs. "I am offering you the job of Pookie's dog walker."

Lulu didn't think much of a dog that couldn't even be bothered to open her eyes. But she very much liked the twelve dollars and fifty cents that she would be paid every week to walk her. Remembering, as she did now and then, the manners she had learned from Mr. B, Lulu said to Pookie's mommy, "Thank you. I accept. I'll see you at six thirty-two on Monday morning."

chapter seven

The third house Lulu stopped at was a haunted-looking house, its yard overgrown with half-dead bushes and weeds, and all kinds of wrecked and rusted and ratty old furniture, pots, bikes, toys, and other junk piled helter-skelter on its sagging front porch. The skinny man and woman who answered the door in matching warm-up suits and baseball caps greeted Lulu warmly and then started poking around in the mess on the porch, with Mister explaining, "Our dog is in there somewhere," and Missus explaining, "Cordelia loves to hide."

Since Mister and Missus seemed to be having trouble finding Cordelia, Lulu joined in the hunt for the hidden dog, whose tail or ear or eye or leg would make a brief appearance, then once again vanish. Finally, Lulu, desperately trying to grab some part of Cordelia, instead knocked a broken-down bike off the top of the pile, which was followed by an avalanche of water-soaked books, chipped dishes, several window screens with holes, and . . . one yapping dog.

Lulu covered her head with her
hand to keep it from being bopped by
a falling screen. With the other hand
she reached out for Cordelia.

"Gotcha!" said Lulu.

"Good job!" said Mister and Missus,
who patted her shoulder and told her
she was hired.

And Lulu, handing them back their
dog, said to Mister and Missus, "I'll
see you Monday morning at
six thirty-four."

time-out

$\mathcal{I}$ can tell you already have questions for me, and I think I know what they are. So, why don't we take a time-out and get them over with?

Shouldn't Lulu's mom and her dad stop her from trying to walk three dogs at once?

 They should, but they won't. Lulu is hard to stop.

 What happened to Fleischman— didn't you say he'd be hanging around a lot?

 I did, and he will be. Don't be in such a rush.

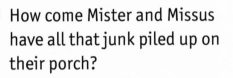

Q: How come Mister and Missus
have all that junk piled up on
their porch?

A: Beats me.
I've been wondering the
exact same thing.

Q: What is it Lulu wants to
buy with all this money
she's earning?

A: I really don't feel like
discussing that right now.

chapter eight

On Sunday night, before bedtime,
Lulu carefully set the alarm clock for 6:25.
She picked out the clothes she wanted
to wear—so she wouldn't have to think
about them in the morning. She tracked
down her disappeared sneakers and
carefully placed them next to her bed—so
she wouldn't have to go looking for them
in the morning. She even, to save a few
seconds, squeezed some toothpaste onto
her toothbrush—so she wouldn't have
to squeeze toothpaste in the morning.

She figured that she could be dressed, washed, and tooth-brushed in three minutes and fifteen seconds on Monday morning, which would leave her forty-five seconds to eat some cold cereal, and one whole minute to run to Brutus's house.

Lulu was feeling extremely pleased with her plan. So, after saying good night to her mom and her dad and her pet goldfish and the photo of Mr. B that hung on her wall, she sang herself to sleep with a money song:

Danny, Donnie, Dustin, Dave.
How much money will I save?
Ava, Amy, Ann, Annette.
How much money will I get?
Money! Money! Money!
Money! Money!

Lulu expected to have some merry money dreams that night, but instead she dreamed all night about—guess who?—Fleischman. He was standing outside her front door and shaking his head and saying over and over again, "THREE dogs you're walking? Mistake. A big mistake."

chapter nine

Lulu woke up at 6:25, and for the first five minutes her plan worked perfectly. Dressed and washed and tooth-brushed in exactly, EXACTLY, three minutes and fifteen seconds? Check. Ate a bowl of cereal in precisely, PRECISELY, forty-five seconds? Check. Arrived at Brutus's house in one minute flat and rang the bell at 6:30 sharp? Check, and double-check, and for good measure check again. This girl was GOLDEN.

Brutus was happy to see her, so happy he knocked her flat down on the rug, slobbered all over her face, and thumped his tail. Brutus's owner was proud. "Is that cute or what?"

Lulu, who most definitely did not think it was cute, replied, "It's what." And then she stood up, wiped off, attached the leash to Brutus's collar, and—she was running a little bit late—was out the door, heading to Pookie's house.

I mean, she was TRYING to head to Pookie's house. Brutus was heading in a different direction. She pulled. He pulled.

She pulled. He pulled. She pulled.
He pulled harder, making Lulu bang
into a tree.

Which gave her, along with a bump on
her knee, an idea.

Lulu began to wrap the long leash
around the trunk of the tree, wrapping it
so tightly around and around and around
the trunk that Brutus, two houses down,

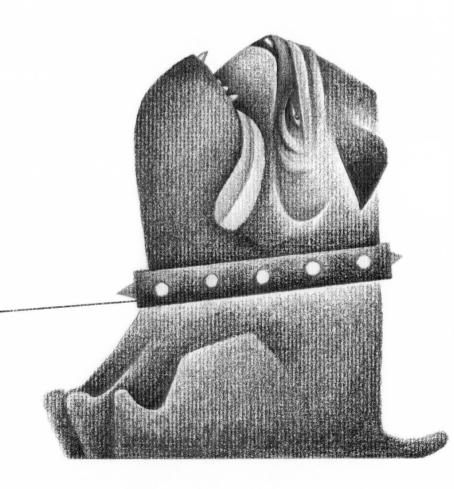

couldn't pull her anymore or go any farther. Dog and girl had stopped moving, and—across the space between them— they were glaring at each other most ferociously.

"We're doing it my way, Brutus," Lulu announced in her bossiest voice.

"That won't happen," came the instant reply. But in case you're thinking that Brutus was speaking, you can think again. The voice Lulu heard belonged—big surprise!—to Fleischman.

Just the person she didn't want to see.

"You're just the person I didn't want to see," said Lulu.

"Dog biscuits," Fleischman mysteriously replied.

"Dog biscuits yourself," said Lulu, and went back to staring ferociously at Brutus: girl and dog still standing still—girl under a tree, holding on to one end of the leash, and dog, two houses down, attached to the other end—in a situation grown-ups call an impasse. (A complicated word that means neither one's going to do what the other one wants him to do.)

"If you're wanting Brutus to walk with you nicely to Pookie's house," said Fleischman, "you need a dog-biscuit trail for him to follow. And since I'm thinking you don't have any dog biscuits in your pockets, we'll use mine."

Fleischman walked over to Brutus and dropped a biscuit in front of his nose, which Brutus gladly and instantly gulped down. Then Fleischman turned around and walked back toward Lulu, dropping biscuit after biscuit on the ground, creating a tasty dog-biscuit trail that Brutus eagerly followed, gulping down biscuits. Soon thereafter, Fleischman and Brutus were standing next to Lulu under the tree.

"And now if you'll just unwind the leash from that tree trunk," Fleischman told Lulu, "we can get going."

Lulu, with Brutus on the leash and Fleischman walking ahead of them dropping biscuits, arrived without further

fuss at Pookie's house. Lulu waited for
Fleischman to leave. He didn't. Instead
he said, "If you let me hold Brutus's leash
while you go inside and pick up Pookie,
we'll save some time."

"*We're* not saving time," said Lulu. "*I* am
saving time. So wait out here with Brutus,
if you want to, but I'm warning you,
Fleischman, don't get any ideas."

"I'm not getting any ideas," said
Fleischman. "I'm just happy to help.
Happy and pleased and proud and
delighted and honored and . . ."

"Quiet, Fleischman!" said Lulu in a voice
that could shut up a city. "And stop being
so happy."

chapter ten

Lulu was out of Pookie's house in twenty seconds flat, promising Pookie's mommy that she would be careful not to hurt the fuzzball's feelings. Holding Pookie with one of her hands and Brutus's leash with the other, Lulu was hurrying over to Cordelia's when Pookie—finally!—opened her eyes and wiggled. And then kind of squeaked. Then wiggled and squeaked some more. Lulu understood that this was Pookie's way of saying it was time to do what she was supposed to do. Which meant that Lulu needed to stop immediately and set down Pookie underneath a tree. Which she did and then said, in a not-too-patient voice, "Okay, let's get this over with. Do what you're supposed to do—right now."

"She won't if you talk like that," said a voice that belonged—do I have to tell you?—to Fleischman. "She needs to be coaxed."

"I am not a person who coaxes," Lulu told Fleischman. Then, bending down, she repeated, "Pookie—right now!"

Except that when she spoke, instead of the POOK part rhyming with DUKE, Lulu forgot and rhymed it with—uh-oh!—BOOK. Which turned out to be a mistake. A big mistake.

Pookie, yelping, leaped up in the air,
and instead of falling back down again,
she attached herself—by her teeth—to
Lulu's jean jacket. Lulu tried pulling her
off. Pookie hung on. Lulu tried pushing
her off. Pookie hung on. Lulu tried
shaking her off, but the once-lazy fuzzball
wouldn't let go, hanging on by her teeth
and somehow yelping at the same time,
which isn't that easy.

All of a sudden—out of the blue—
Lulu began to hear music. What was
this music? Where was it coming from?
Well—what do you know!—there was
Fleischman, who had taken his flute from
his backpack and was toot-toot-tootling
tunes into Pookie's ear.

"Fleischman!" yelled Lulu, still pulling
and pushing and trying to shake off
Pookie. "Cut out the concert!"

"This isn't a concert," said Fleischman. "This is coaxing."

Lulu watched with amazement as the yelping Pookie stopped yelping and hanging on by her teeth to Lulu's jacket. Instead, while Fleischman kept playing, Pookie let herself drop to the ground where, quietly squatting under the big leafy tree, she quickly did what she was supposed to do.

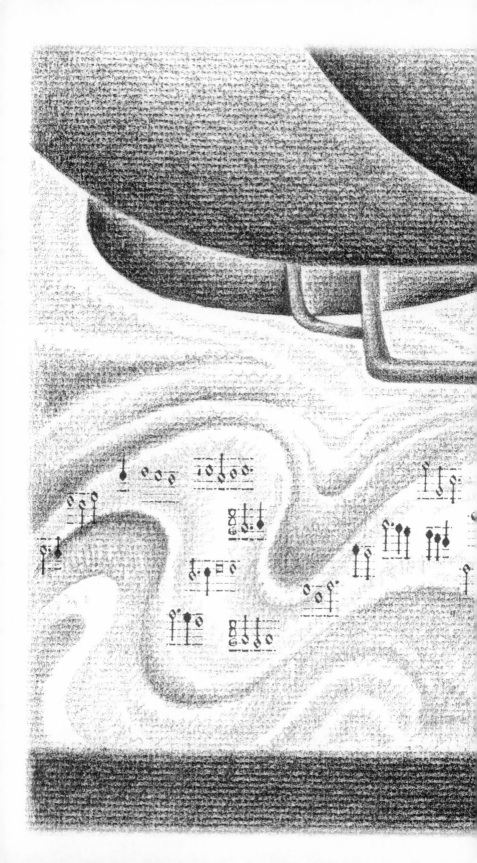

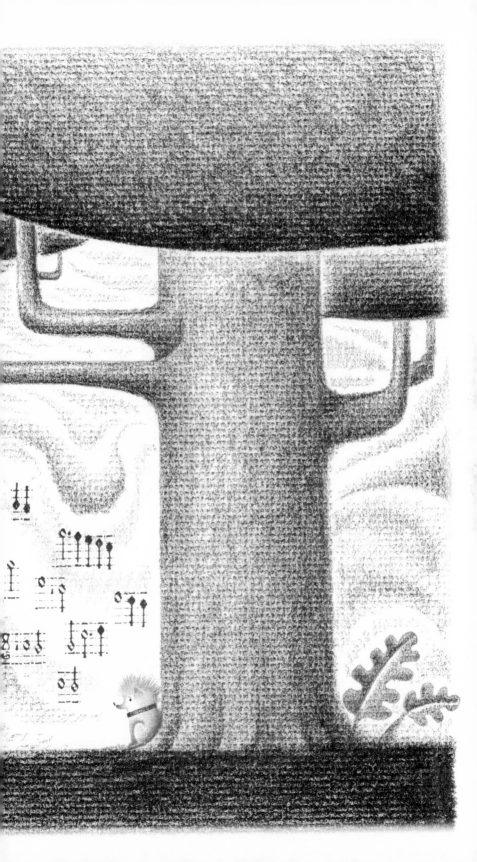

(Why is everyone saying that Pookie "did what she was supposed to do"? From now on I am going to just say "pooped.")

Fleischman whipped out a pooper-scooper, cleaned up the little mess, picked up Pookie, and handed her to Lulu. "Don't thank me," he told her, even though Lulu hadn't said a word. "Actually, I should be thanking you. I should be thanking you for letting me . . ."

"I don't want to hear it, Fleischman!" roared Lulu. "I really, really, really DON'T WANT TO HEAR IT. Now, out of my way, I'm seriously behind schedule."

time-out

I just this minute realized, even though I've already told you that Brutus is a great big, bad-breathed brute and that Pookie is a tiny, lazy, white fuzzball, I haven't yet said that—along with loving to hide—Cordelia is a long, low, short-legged, hot-dog-looking dog whose animal name starts with *d*, except I can't remember what comes after the *d*. Oh, and one more thing about Cordelia: She is very—and I mean VERY—vain.

chapter eleven

Lulu, filled with impatience, was
standing on Mister and Missus's porch—
and she was late. Fleischman was waiting
patiently under a tree. He was holding on
to Pookie, who immediately fell asleep,
and gently patting Brutus, who promptly
pooped. Mister and Missus weren't upset
about Lulu's being late, because they
were busy looking for Cordelia. Who, even
with Lulu's help, could not be found.
Fleischman watched Mister and Missus
and Lulu calling "Cordelia, Cordelia," as
they poked and prodded the junk pile
on the porch. And then, because it was
getting too late and even though Lulu
scowled a stay-out-of-this scowl, he
joined them. Handing the two dogs to

Lulu, Fleischman knelt by the pile of junk and started speaking softly in a language that nobody else on that front porch knew. Well, nobody but Cordelia, because as soon as he started talking, she came popping out of the pile and, yapping blissfully, went waddling over to Fleischman.

"It's Cordelia!" shouted Mister.

"It's Cordelia!" shouted Missus.

"It's time," Lulu announced, "for me to go." Quickly taking over, she attached Cordelia's leash to Cordelia's collar, and holding on to all three dogs—Pookie against her chest, the others on leashes— she turned to Fleischman, nodded, and said, "I'm leaving."

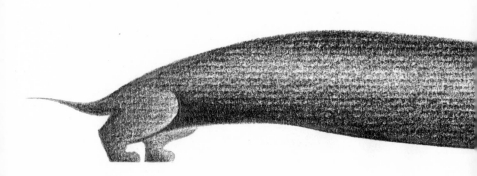

(That nod was maybe Lulu saying thank you. Or maybe not.)

Fleischman, though not invited, was leaving with Lulu. But Mister and Missus first had two questions to ask. What kind of language did Fleischman speak to Cordelia? And what exactly did he say to her?

"I spoke in German," Fleischman explained, "because Cordelia's a dachshund, and dachshunds are German. I also know how to talk to French poodles in French." Then he told Mister and Missus what he said to Cordelia to make her come out of hiding, but I really don't feel like discussing that right now.

chapter twelve

Six and a half minutes later, evening up with Brutus and Pookie, Cordelia pooped.

chapter thirteen

Lulu needed to get back home, or else she'd be late for school. But she also needed to bring the dogs back to their owners. "I can do that," said Fleischman. "I don't have school today. They're giving me the day off because I'm so smart."

Lulu knew she should thank him, but she really, really, really wanted to stomp him. Wouldn't you?

Still, as Fleischman went off with Cordelia and Pookie and Brutus, and Lulu pulled up her socks and hurried home, she forgot about all the difficulties of the morning and thought about all the money she'd already earned. Which inspired her to sing a money song.

Howie, Harry, Harvey, Hank.
Lots of money for my bank.
Goldie, Gracie, Gladys, Glor.
Lots of money for my drawer.

Money!

Money!

Money!

Money!

Money!

(Lulu thinks it's okay to use the name "Glor" to rhyme with "drawer" because, she says, Glor is a nickname for Gloria. I'm not so sure.)

After school on Monday, Lulu remembered all the difficulties of the morning and decided she'd have to SPEND some money to make some. She went to the market and bought the cheapest dog

biscuits she could find. She went to the toy store and bought, for only sixty-nine cents plus tax, a plastic toy flute. And

then she went to the library and took
out, from the language section, an easy-
looking book called *Beginner's German*.

She figured it wouldn't take much to learn
what she needed to learn to make the
dogs behave. She figured that she would
do just fine without Fleischman.

chapter fourteen

She didn't. Brutus hated the taste of Lulu's cheap dog biscuits. Pookie yelped when Lulu toot-toot-tootled the toy plastic flute in her ear. And Cordelia, who either did not understand or pretended to not understand Lulu's German, kept right on hiding. In other words, Tuesday was just as bad as Monday. Fleischman, who was hanging around, asked Lulu if he could help her. Lulu sighed and said a grouchy, "Okay."

chapter fifteen

Lulu bought better dog biscuits, practiced harder on the flute, and memorized saying in German (though it made her want to throw up), "You are the bestest, most beautiful dog in the world." But Wednesday was worse than Monday and Tuesday combined because Brutus wouldn't start walking, and Pookie wouldn't stop yelping, and Cordelia hid so well that she couldn't be found, in addition to which Brutus missed and pooped all over Lulu's foot—maybe on purpose. Fleischman, who was hanging around, asked if he could help. Lulu sighed and said a grouchy, "Okay."

chapter sixteen

On Thursday, after a morning TWICE as bad as Monday and Tuesday and Wednesday combined, Lulu told Fleischman she'd hire him as her assistant. She said she would pay him thirteen dollars a week.

chapter seventeen

Thirteen dollars a week—is that fair? Let me figure this out. Lulu is getting twelve dollars and fifty cents a week for Cordelia, and another twelve dollars and fifty cents for Pookie, and a great big fifteen dollars a week for Brutus. Add all these up and she gets, every week . . . she gets, every single week . . . she gets, every single week—I'm close, I'm close, I'm almost there—she gets, every single week, forty whole dollars!

And she wants to give Fleischman,
who works just as hard, maybe harder, a
measly thirteen dollars every week? That
doesn't seem one bit fair to me but—hold
it!—listen to what Fleischman is saying.

"I don't want your money, Lulu. I am
happy, delighted, thrilled to help you for

free. It's truly my pleasure to serve you, to . . ."

"Fleischman, stop it right now!" Lulu roared. "Or I'm throwing up, right now, on your perfect sneakers."

Fleischman shrugged his shoulders and stopped it right now.

chapter eighteen

On Friday and for the next two weeks, Lulu—along with Fleischman—walked the dogs. They each took turns making dog-biscuit trails for Brutus. They each took turns coaxing Pookie by tooting the flute. And they each took turns saying the most flattering things in German to Cordelia to persuade her to come out of her hiding place. And as long as Fleischman was there, the dogs behaved.

Lulu didn't have much to say to Fleischman. She didn't want Fleischman saying much to her. But on their third Friday together, after the dogs were returned to their owners, Fleischman tapped Lulu's elbow and said to her quietly, "We make a good team."

Big mistake.

Lulu stopped walking and started scowling at Fleischman. She put her hands on her hips. She narrowed her eyes. "Fleischman," she said to Fleischman, "I

want you to listen, and listen carefully.
We aren't a team. We will NEVER be a
team. I'm the dog-walking boss, and you
are only my assistant. ¿*Comprendez?*"

(*Comprendez* is Spanish for "Do you
understand?" But why, you may very
well ask, did she say it in Spanish? I
really don't feel like discussing that
right now.)

Fleischman nodded his head to show
that yes, he understood. And then he
turned and silently headed home.

chapter nineteen

Patrick, Preston, Paulie, Pete.
Money for my special treat.
Julie, Jackie, Jenny, Joan.
Money for myself alone.
Money! Money! Money!
Money! Money!

Lulu sang a money song as she hurried to Brutus's house on Monday morning. Fleischman was usually waiting for her outside. Except today there wasn't any Fleischman. Lulu gave him a minute. And then she gave him two minutes. And then she gave him three minutes—

"Three strikes and you're out," Lulu said to no one in particular. After which she announced, "So what if Fleischman isn't here. I'm going to walk these dogs all by myself. I know I can walk these dogs all by myself." She took a deep breath and said out loud, sounding a lot more sure than maybe she was, "I'M READY TO WALK THESE DOGS ALL BY MYSELF."

And I have to admit that, for a little while, Lulu actually looked as if she were ready.

Because:

Brutus followed obediently as Lulu dropped biscuits and made him a dog-biscuit trail.

Pookie listened politely as Lulu coaxingly tooted her flute, after which she (as in Pookie, not Lulu) pooped.

And Cordelia, after Lulu said some gooey blah-blah-blahs to her in German, was persuaded to waddle out of her hiding place.

But as soon as Mister and Missus waved good-bye to their Cordelia and closed the front door, the morning got worse than it ever had been before.

Lulu, standing under a tree, said to
the dogs, in one of her bossiest voices,
"Okay, let's move it—Brutus! Cordelia!
Pookie!"—except she forgot, and rhymed
the POOK part with BOOK. (This, as you
may remember, hurts Pookie's feelings.
Which, as you may remember, you don't
want to do.)

Pookie, leaping up high in the air, fastened her pointy teeth onto Lulu's jean jacket, holding on tight and yelping at the same time, while Cordelia slipped out of her collar and went dashing back onto the porch, where she hid herself deep, deep down in the pile of junk. As all this was going on, big Brutus, who wasn't as dumb as he looked, circled wildly around and around the tree trunk, wrapping his leash around it just as tightly as Lulu had done on their very first walk together. And Lulu, who had been leaning against the tree as she tried (and kept failing) to shake off Pookie, discovered—too late! too late!—that she had been totally tied, by Brutus's leash, to the trunk!

Totally, utterly, absolutely, embarrassingly, humiliatingly tied.

She couldn't move her arms. She couldn't move her legs. She couldn't chase after Cordelia or shake off Pookie. And she certainly couldn't untangle herself from the leash, still attached at the other end to Brutus, who was standing just out of her reach, triumphantly woofing.

(And if you find it hard to believe when I tell you that Brutus tied up Lulu on purpose, remember who's in charge of this story—me!)

Lulu wriggled and wriggled, but she couldn't get herself loose. So, after a while, she stopped wriggling and began to think about what she could do to get loose. And after a longer while, she started wriggling some more. Until finally, after feeling that she had been tied forever to the trunk of that tree, Lulu saw—well, you know who she saw— Fleischman.

Yup, there he was, good old Fleischman, strolling slowly down the street, playing "You Are My Sunshine" on his flute.

Just the person Lulu did not want to see.

Just the person Lulu needed to see.

Just in time to take another time-out.

think we ought to discuss what's going on here.

I don't feel one bit sorry for Lulu—do you? You remember I said back in Chapter One that, since she met Mr. B, Lulu wasn't as big a pain as she'd been. And not nearly as rude. But she sure was being extremely rude to Fleischman. Rude! Rude! Rude! And also ungrateful! For Fleischman helped her over and over, and said he was happy to help, and didn't even want money from her for helping. And all Lulu did was boss him around and threaten that she would throw up on him, plus she wouldn't be his friend, or even his teammate. Maybe she needs to keep staying tied to that tree until she says, "I'm sorry, Fleischman."

Wait, I think she just whispered, "I'm sorry, Fleischman."

chapter twenty

Well, it turns out that Lulu didn't exactly say, "I'm sorry, Fleischman." What she actually said to him was, "Untie me, Fleischman," followed ten or twenty seconds later by a growly sounding "please."

Fleischman stopped tooting and stood right in front of the very grumpy, very tied-up Lulu. "*Teammates* untie each other," Fleischman told her. "But I'm not your teammate."

"An assistant unties his boss,"
said Lulu, giving Fleischman one of
her fiercer glares. "And, Fleischman,
you're my assistant—so untie me."

"In case you didn't notice," said
Fleischman, who wasn't one bit
bothered by Lulu's glare, "I am
not your assistant anymore. I quit
last Friday."

"A person can't quit on Friday," said Lulu, "just by not coming back to work on Monday. A person has to say 'I quit' to quit."

"Okay, then," Fleischman said to Lulu. "I quit." And then he walked slowly past her, playing some more of "You Are My Sunshine" on his flute.

With Lulu loudly yelling, "You get back here, Fleischman! You get back here now!"

time-out

think that I need to mention that, by this time, Lulu and Fleischman were quite late for school. But although, for several hours, they weren't where they should have been, not one single person noticed they weren't there. Not Lulu's teacher. Not Fleischman's teacher. Not any of their classmates. No one!

Plus, nobody walking down that street—and lots of people were—seemed to notice that Lulu was tied to a tree. And not just tied to a tree, but wriggling and yelling and making quite a remarkable fuss. (In actual life this almost never could happen. In the stories I write, things like this happen a lot. Deal with it.)

Oh, and I think I should mention that, by this time, Pookie had fallen sound asleep, let go of Lulu's jacket, and dropped to the grass, where she curled in a tight white fuzzball and yawned a great big yawn and kept on sleeping. And that Cordelia, bored with hiding under the junk pile—with nobody trying to find her, it wasn't much fun—waddled over to Pookie, flopped down right beside her, and soon was snoring very loudly, in German. And that Brutus, his heavy head drooping lower and lower, was just as deep asleep as the rest of them. Except for Lulu, of course, who was wide awake and still screaming, "Get back here, Fleischman! Now!"

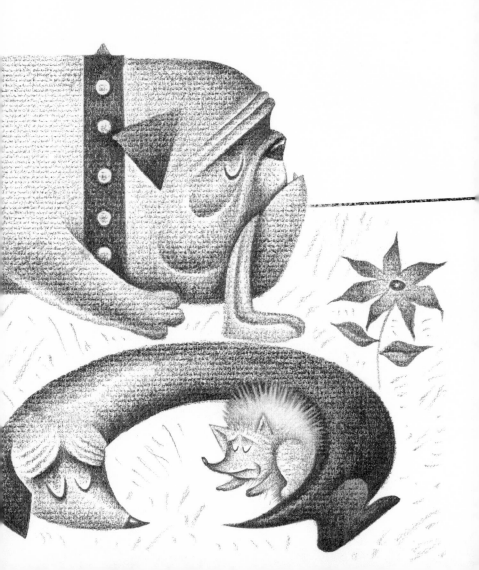

chapter twenty-one

Fleischman got back there.

"Okay, I'll untie you," Fleischman said to Lulu. "But only if you'll explain how come you hate me."

"Oh, I can do that," said Lulu. "That'll be easy." And then she gave him ten different explanations:

"You're always eating carrots.

"You never eat anything that's bad for you.

"Your sneakers look like they just came out of a store.

"You play an actual flute instead of a toy one.

"You wear that ugly T-shirt that says,

(I didn't mention this earlier because that T-shirt makes *me* want to throw up.)

"You have this really, really annoying smile.

"You keep saying things like you can speak German and French.

"You keep saying things like 'I'm honored and thrilled to serve you.'

"You got a day off from school because you're so smart.

"You're a total expert on dogs—and you don't even *have* a dog.

"All the moms and the dads in the world think you're perfect, and maybe you are, and how can a person not hate a person who's perfect?

(Okay, so I made a mistake. Lulu gave him *eleven* explanations. But forget about that—right now I am anxious to hear what Fleischman will say. Aren't you?)

chapter twenty-two

Except, for a while, Fleischman didn't say anything. He was busy untying Lulu from the tree, which turned out to be much harder than he, or she, or even I had ever expected. Before he was finished, however, he took a deep breath and said to Lulu, "It's not fair to hate a person because he's perfect." And then he added, so softly she barely could hear him, "Besides—I'm not perfect. I am *so* not perfect."

So not perfect? Fleischman was *so* not perfect? Hmmm.

"Keep talking, Fleischman," Lulu said to Fleischman, looking pleased for the very first time that day. "Stop trying to untie me, and tell me more." Fleischman stopped untying and told her more.

"I don't change my underpants every single day.

"You wouldn't believe the mess that's under my bed.

"I'm scared of the dark.

"I'm also scared—make that

ABSOLUTELY TERRIFIED—of crawly-creatures like caterpillars and worms.

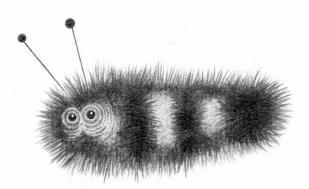

"I can only speak German to dachshunds and French to poodles. Whenever I try to speak German or French to humans they can never understand me.

"I play the flute because I already tried and couldn't play the violin, the piano, the guitar, the clarinet, the drums, and the *gusli*." (The what? The WHAT? I really don't feel like discussing that right now.)

Lulu kept listening cheerfully until Fleischman was done telling more and went back to untying. And then she— looking even more cheerful—said, "Terrified of crawly creatures! Smelly underwear! Can't play the *gusli*!"

Fleischman shrugged. Lulu kept on talking. "But what about all that goody-goody stuff—the carrots, the sneakers, the smile? Plus being so honored and thrilled? Plus being so smart?"

"That's who I am," said Fleischman. "I can't help it. Just like you can't help"—and all of a sudden he started to speak in a very loud voice—"that you are really, really dumb about dogs. Plus, you certainly aren't the nicest girl in the world."

(Whoa! Listen to Fleischman! Who ever knew that he could talk that way!)

Lulu glared at Fleischman.
Fleischman glared at Lulu. But
instead of an impasse, they had
a conversation—a quite noisy
conversation that lasted the rest
of the morning and all of the
afternoon. There was yelling (from
Lulu) and crying (from Fleischman)
and yelling (from Fleischman) and
crying (from Lulu) and (from both
of them) much stamping of feet.
But when they were finished with
all of that, Lulu and Fleischman
shook each other's hand.

chapter twenty-three

From that day on, Lulu and Fleischman were more than boss and assistant and more than teammates. They were, in fact, partners, with Lulu offering Fleischman (and making him take) exactly half of the money she earned walking dogs, and promising to teach him (for only ten dollars) how not to be scared of caterpillars and worms, plus whispering (in a voice he hardly could hear, but at least she said it) that although she had no wish to be the nicest girl in the world— boring! too boring!—she would try her very best to be nicer to him.

(Somewhere deep in his forest, Mr. B is slowly nodding his head and smiling.)

Fleischman, in return, promised that he'd give away the shirt that says I'M HERE TO BRING SOME HAPPINESS INTO YOUR LIFE, teach her (for only ten dollars) to understand dogs, try his very best to stop saying how honored and thrilled and delighted and smart he was, and work on smiling a less annoying smile.

Did Lulu stop hating Fleischman? Yes, she did. Did Lulu stop being rude to him? Yes, she did. Was Lulu now willing to talk with him while they walked the dogs together on weekday mornings? Yes, she was. And so, did Fleischman and Lulu finally turn into New Best Friends? No, they did not.

You want a happy ending? Read *Cinderella*. This story has only sort of a happy ending. Because Fleischman is still too annoying for Lulu to love. And Lulu is still too fierce for Fleischman to love. They respect each other. They count on each other. They're partners and dog-walking buddies. If one of them got tied up, the other would help. But unless they turn into totally different people, I'm pretty sure they won't be New Best Friends.

Still, the last time I saw them together they were walking Brutus and Pookie and Cordelia. Lulu was trying to kick some dirt on Fleischman's perfect sneakers. Fleischman was shaking a carrot in Lulu's face. And as they got near the end of the street I could hear them loudly singing this money song:

Larry, Liam, Lester, Lou.
All this money for us two.
Cathy, Carly, Chloe, Claire.

All this money we can share.
Money! Money! Money!
Money! Money!

the last time-out

I'm sure you have some more questions for me, and I think I know what they are. So I guess I should try to help you find the answers.

Q: How come some moms (like Fleischman's mom) change their last name when they marry, and some moms don't?

A: Different moms are going to have different reasons, so go ask your own mom why she didn't or did. And how come, if she changed her last name, she didn't give you a first name like Anderson, or Kelly, or even Fleischman.

Q: Why in the world did Lulu say, "*¿Comprendez?*," rather than saying, "Do you understand?"

A: She was hoping that Fleischman would think that she was able to speak Spanish. She actually can't.

 What did Fleischman say the first time he talked to Cordelia in German?

A: He told her she had won first prize in the International Dachshund Beauty Contest. She actually hadn't.

Q: Is there a musical instrument called the *gusli*?

A: There is. But only a Fleischman would want to play it.

Q: So what is this superspecial thing that Lulu wants to buy, this thing that she says she will want FOREVER and ALWAYS, this thing that her mom and her dad keep saying (with many sorries and sighs) they cannot afford, this expensive and wonderful thing that Lulu will someday be able to pay for with the money she has earned by walking the dogs?

A: I really don't feel like discussing that right now, but if you insist, I guess we'll have to go into overtime.

overtime

Q: *Okay,* so now we're in overtime, and I'm asking you once more: What is this superspecial thing that Lulu is going to buy when she earns enough money?

A: What Lulu is hoping to buy, what Lulu is planning to buy, what Lulu is GOING to buy is . . . a seat on a spaceship. She wants to be the very first kid in all the entire world to take a journey into outer space.

Q: That's impossible, right?

A: Impossible? What do you mean, impossible? Have you forgotten who is writing this story?

Q: But wouldn't a seat on a spaceship cost at least a million dollars?

A: No, a seat on a spaceship would cost at least TWENTY-FIVE million dollars. But Lulu convinced the people in charge to take away some zeros so she'll only have to pay twenty-five hundred dollars.

Q: But if Lulu makes forty dollars a week, and she's giving half to Fleischman, won't it take her forever to earn enough money?

A: Not really. Lulu says that it's going to take two years and twenty-one weeks of walking the dogs. Which definitely is worth it, she says, to be the very first kid in outer space.

Q: The first kid in outer space: Won't that be lonely?

A: Actually, no. Lulu says that as long as he absolutely understands that he'll just be the SECOND kid in outer space, she is going to save a seat for Fleischman.

Turn the page to join Lulu for a third
adventure full of hilarious hijinks,
delightful twists, and a
top-secret mission!

JUDITH VIORST *illustrated by* KEVIN CORNELL

From Atheneum Books for Young Readers

STOP! *Don't begin the I need to tell you. And I think I'd better*

This isn't a book about Lulu's Mysterious Mission. It's actually about Lulu's Babysitter. And that's what I wanted to call it except two kids that I know, Benjamin and Nathaniel, kept telling me that *Lulu's Babysitter* was a really boring title. Which means that the name of this book has absolutely nothing at all to do with the story I'm writing.

You have now been warned!

Wait! Now that I have warned you,

first chapter just yet. There's something
tell it to you right now.

I am feeling a tiny bit guilty. Like maybe it isn't fair to trick readers like that. Like maybe there ought to be a law that what's INSIDE a book has to somehow match up with the NAME of the book. So maybe—I'm not *promising*, but just maybe—I'll put in some stuff about a Mysterious Mission.

Meanwhile, either return this book or keep reading. You'll find out what happens when Lulu meets up with Ms. Sonia Sofia Solinsky, who is definitely not your Mary Poppins–type babysitter.

But first let's go find Lulu, who is in the living room screeching "No! No! No!" although she doesn't screech much anymore. However, the news she was hearing from her mom and her dad was so utterly, totally SHOCKING that it not only started her screeching but almost shocked her into throwing one of her heel-kicking, arm-waving, on-the-floor tantrums. Lulu, however, thinks of herself

as too grown-up now to throw tantrums. Which also means she thinks of herself as grown-up enough to go with her mom and her dad on the trip they just told her that they would be taking WITHOUT HER.

When Lulu had finished screeching, she fiercely glared at her mom and her dad and asked them—in a not-too-nice voice—these questions:

"How can you have a good time if I'm not there?"

And "Who's going to take care of me, and how can you be positive that this person won't kidnap me and hold me for ransom?"

And "Or maybe she'll stop feeding me and start yelling at me and hitting me and locking me down in the basement with the rats." (Okay, that isn't technically a question.)

When Lulu was done, her mom and her dad looked at each other, then answered—very carefully. For even though their daughter wasn't the serious pain in the butt that she used to be, she wasn't the easiest girl in the world to be parents to when she didn't get her way.

"First of all," said Lulu's dad, "there are no rats in our basement. As a matter of fact, we don't even HAVE a basement."

"But even if we did," said Lulu's mom, "we'd never hire a sitter who'd lock you up in it. Or starve you or hit you or yell at you or kidnap you."

"Or," added Lulu's dad, "hold you for ransom."

"And if you were held for ransom," Lulu's mom assured Lulu, patting her oh-so-lovingly on the cheek, "we'd pay whatever it took to get you back."

"But," Lulu pointed out, removing her mom's patting hand from her cheek, "if instead of paying the ransom, you'd let me come with you, this trip of yours would cost a lot less money."

Lulu's dad explained that as much as they loved and adored their precious only child, they wanted to have—for the first time since they'd been parents—a private grown-ups-only vacation together. And that even though they wouldn't be having the kind of fun they had with their fabulous Lulu, they would be having a DIFFERENT kind of fun.

"You mean BETTER fun," grumped Lulu. "You'll have better fun without me. And you won't even care when I get sick and die."

Lulu's mom started crying at the thought of poor little Lulu, left behind and dead of a broken heart. "Maybe . . . ," she sniffled to Lulu's dad, "maybe we ought to stay home. Or take her with us. Maybe we are being too unkind."

It's at this point in every argument that Lulu almost always gets her way because her mom and her dad just cannot BEAR it when their darling is displeased. It's right at this point that Lulu almost always gets what she wants because her mom and her dad give up and give in. Except on those rare occasions—like now, for instance— when they try NOT to.

Lulu's dad cleared his throat, and in a strong, firm voice replied to Lulu's mom. "No," he said. "We're going. She's staying. THAT'S what we decided and"—he took a deep breath—"we're sticking to it."

He then turned to Lulu and said, "But you don't have a thing to worry about, dearest darling. Because, after much research, we've hired the best babysitter in town—maybe the world—to take care of you the week that we're away."

"Babysitter?" Lulu gasped. "Babysitter? Babysitters sit babies, and I'm no baby."

(Lulu thinks she's no baby because she plays a tough game of Scrabble, goes by herself to the corner store to buy milk, gets good reports from her teachers, earns some money walking dogs, rides a bike with no hands, and has pierced ears. She's also on the softball team, the swim team, and the debate team; has recently started learning the trombone; and is going to be a crossing guard next year. And what Lulu wants to know is why a person who can do all that would need a person called a *baby*sitter.)

"Call her what you want, but her name," Lulu's mom said soothingly, "is Ms. Sonia Sofia Solinsky, a trained professional. And we're sure, dear, that if you, dear, will give her, dear, a chance, dear, the two of you will get along just fine."

"In fact," said Lulu's dad, "she's moving in this afternoon. We'll show her around the house, and maybe you two can start to bond before your mom and I leave tomorrow morning."

(Tomorrow morning? They're leaving tomorrow morning? How come Lulu is only now being told that her mom and her dad are leaving tomorrow morning?

How come she wasn't told earlier? How come she wasn't given time to prepare? As the person who's writing this story, I take full responsibility for this decision. Because anyone who knows Lulu like I know Lulu wouldn't want to give her time to prepare.)

"I'm going up to my room," said Lulu to her mom and her dad. "And maybe I'll come down and maybe I won't. But while I'm up there," she added as she loudly tromped up the stairs, "I'm planning to be very very unhappy."

Up in her room, along with being very very unhappy, Lulu was trying to figure out what to do. Actually, she knew WHAT to do: get rid of the babysitter so her mom and her dad would have no one to leave her with. All she needed to figure out was HOW.

She went to her computer—yes, she has her own computer; she has her own *everything*—and typed in "How To Get Rid of a Babysitter." But nothing too helpful came up, so Lulu started making a list of possibilities, and as she wrote she chanted this little chant:

*Eeny meeny miney mo,
That babysitter's got to go.*

While Lulu was chanting and making her list, the doorbell rang and a voice boomed through the house, a voice that sounded to Lulu like real bad news. "Sonia Sofia Solinsky," it said. "At your service."

Lulu heard the gentle murmurs of her mom and her dad, interspersed with Ms. Solinsky's boom, and the quiet patter of their feet, interspersed with Ms. Solinsky's clomp, and then someone (either her mom or her dad) was knocking softly at her bedroom door, with Ms. Solinsky bellowing, "The eagle has landed, Lulu. Open up."